To Jason

Lives of the Saints

thanks for all the kind words — so good to see you after so many years — wish you all the best for your return,

Nino Ricci

LIVES OF THE SAINTS
Alan Franklin

No Copyright 2022

Black & Red Books
PO Box 02374
Detroit MI 48202
www.BlackandRed.org

Cover and book design: Ralph Franklin

Available from:
Black & Red Books: www.BlackandRed.org

ISBN: 978-1-948501-20-0

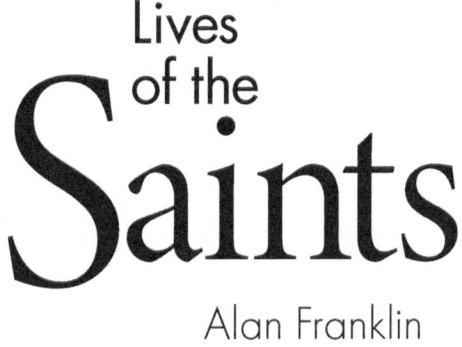

Lives of the Saints

Alan Franklin

Black & Red Books, Detroit

DIS • CON • TENTS

1 Christopher Columbus Steps Ashore
2 An Outpost Of Progress
3 The Socratic Method
4 A Singer Must Die
5 Dialogue I
6 Detention
7 Story
8 Deja Vu
9 Fathers Day
10 The Reprobate
11 Lost Love
12 Hystery
13 And This One From A Young Man At The Front
14 Dialogue II
15 Home Is Where The Hearth Is
16 Fame And Fortune
17 Standoffishness
18 Nothing Ventured, Nothing Lost
19 Yes, But What Are You Feeling?
20 Mine Eyes Have Seen The Glory Of His Terrible Swift Sword
21 The Job
22 Stakhanov In The 21st Century
23 Dialogue III
24 Here Comes The Son
25 Great Expectations
26 The Problem
27 Civilization
28 Employee Of The Month
29 Friendship
30 Mr. Happy Go Lucky
31 The Next-Best Generation
32 I Am Legend
33 Dialogue IV
34 Poetry Is You, Paying Attention
35 I Would Prefer Not To
36 True Story
37 J. D. Salinger Discusses Art And Life With St. Peter
38 Last Words
39 I Dreamed I Was A Returning Deceased War Veteran In My Maidenform Bra
40 I Dreamed I Was A Working Girl
41 What To Do With The Chichimecas
42 Not With A Bang
43 I Dreamed I was Alive
44 The Last Word
45 The End
46 The Other End
AC • KNOW • LEDGE • MENTS

All Photographs By The Author

1 CHRISTOPHER COLUMBUS STEPS ASHORE

... as dogs newly-drowned float by in a delirium of pounding surf, dreaming of a resting place beyond the reach of dog-headed gods. "The difficulty here," says the admiral, his voice hollow as a uniform, "will be to win the hearts and minds of people we will eventually be compelled to roast alive on spits..."

2 AN OUTPOST OF PROGRESS

Several kinds of flatulence engaged us from where we sat: religion, sex, death, etc. The pillagers – I meant to say villagers, or villains – were dressed in antique white ruffles, firearms at the ready, torches held aloft. We had been ordered to evacuate the cemetery but, refusing to forgo our last supper in the palace, had miscalculated the time; now we were taken by surprise as we finished off the last of the horsepiss, mustaches of fine droplets still there where we had held the bottles too long to our lips. Taken out and thrashed, we were impaled one by one, the stench of blood and shit and vomit the inevitable reminder of our own misspent youth. Reaching for a light, I asked someone,
"What made us so?"
"God almighty,
I don't know,"
was his reply. The sun rose over the simmering ruins.
"Nice day for a cookout, though,"
I thought.

3 THE SOCRATIC METHOD

I was told at one point – by one of the interrogators – that I was made of snakes and snails and puppy dogs' tails, though for the longest time I was convinced he had said *snicks* and snails, so that is what I told the monitor when he came to check on my well-being. He nodded politely. "It must be no fun," he called down to me after a while, "being in this filthy pit all day long, prey to every blind, burrowing rodent and unappetizing intestinal parasite that comes down the pike. Still, if you've done nothing wrong, you've nothing to fear from the authorities, eh? Stand up straight when I'm speaking to you. And certainly you have done nothing wrong, am I right?"
"Why, no sir," I said, "nothing."
"So then, you must have nothing to fear from the authorities, is that correct?"
"Uh, yes, sir."
"Then let me hear you say it."
"Say what, sir?"
"That you have nothing to fear from the authorities."
"I have nothing to fear from the authorities, sir."
"And very reassuring it must be to think so, too."
"Yes, sir."
"But that is where you are mistaken, is it not?"
"Mistaken, sir; how so?"
"If you had nothing to fear from the authorities, why then, they would be authorities in name only, would they not? What sort of authority could the authorities expect to wield if everybody thought they had nothing to fear from them? They would say 'Do so-and-so,' and not only would

nobody do so-and-so, many of them would do this or that instead, just out of spite, or churlishness, or some ill-considered adolescent rebellion. And then where would we be? Pandora's Box, man. The Gates of Hell. Soon dissatisfaction and disaffection would rule the roost. Anomie would be the working man's lot, spiritual impoverishment his *bête noire*. Then who would build the great, soaring bridges over the Tigris and Euphrates, the magnificent highway systems that demolish distance and subjugate the landscape everywhere from Nome to no man's land? Before you know it, rivers would be running uphill and the sun would rise in the evening and set in the morning, as it already does in certain benighted reaches of the earthly empire. Is that the kind of life you were looking forward to in your dotage?"

"No, sir."

"I thought not. No, you have everything to fear from the authorities, and that is only as it should be, for therein lies their greatness. If God had not intended for us to eat our animal brethren, why then would he have made them out of meat, and not sand, or pebbles, or bracken?"

4 **A SINGER MUST DIE**

Do you have any last requests? they said. Yes, I said, I'd like peace on earth and goodwill toward men. What about women? they asked. No, I said, thanks, but I don't want any women. That's not what we meant, they said; we meant, what about good will toward women? Well, why not, while we're at it, I answered. Children? They offered. Of course, I said, feeling expansive, dogs and cats, too. What about vermin, they said, since we seem to be tending in that direction? I don't know, I replied, is that a little too much? Why stint now, they said; you'll be dead before you know it – now's no time to hold back. Of course, you're right, I said. I have been a little selfish in my time, a little self-absorbed. That's why we're shooting you, they said. If only I'd thought of this when I was younger, I said, when there was still hope for improvement. It's never too late to change course for the better, they said; you won't regret it in days to come. In days to come I'll be dead, I said. They nodded sagely and tied the blindfold around my head. Why do they always do that? I asked; cover the eyes I mean. Habit as much as anything, they said; it's just the way it's always been done. There's something to be said for tradition, I said. Do you really think so? they replied.

5 DIALOGUE I

And what happens when you don't take the medication?
I'm a danger to myself and others.
Is that your opinion or someone else's?
I think we're in agreement on this one.
What happened before you had the medication?
I would eviscerate things with my teeth.
What kinds of things?
Moles. Voles. Shrews.
Nothing larger?
No, but it was only a matter of time.
Oh?
I fantasized. The cat. My little brother.
Do you think you really would have done that?
Maybe not the cat – what does she know, it's not her fault.
And your little brother?
Is a swine – I despise him. I'd be doing him a favor.
Why do you say that?
His life is a torment, so he torments others.
You?
He wishes.
What are you so angry about?
I'm not angry.
You sound angry.
No, what I sound is disgusted. There's a difference.
And what is that difference?
I would've thought as a shrink you could figure that one out for yourself.

But I'm asking you.
No comment. Next question.
Alright, what about your parents?
What about my parents?
Tell me about them.
They're dolts. Well-meaning dolts, but dolts.
It must be hard being you.
Better than being you.
Do you think my life is so bad?
You're an asshole. And I don't even think you're well meaning.
I'm here to help you.
Okay, then sign me out.
I can't. There are rules; you know that.
See what I mean? You're an asshole.
I'm an asshole because I won't break the rules for you?
That's one reason.
And the others?
Because you're like some creepy gynecologist of the mind. You get your jollies lording it over women you pretend to care about.
Pretty sophisticated thinking for a teenager.
Thanks for reminding me – I almost forgot about the condescension.
Are you finished?
And you dye your hair.
Many men dye their hair nowadays.
I know. It's pathetic.
You dye *your* hair.
I'm not trying to hang on to the last miserable vestiges of my youth.
What are you trying to do with it?
I'm trying to get over it.
Why?
Who wants to be young in your world?
Other generations have certainly had it worse than yours.
Other generations didn't have to live in a world where *everything's* for sale – even some shrink's phony compassion.
You know I'm not going to justify my fees to you.
I don't see how you could.
This is not about the money.
Of course it's about the money. Everything's about the money.

Well, I think we've gone about as far as we can for this session.
What, you're not going to try and fuck me?
Not today I don't think.
You don't think I'm fuckable?
It's not about what I think – our time's up for this week.
Oh, I get it – you left the viagra in your other pants. Just as well, I guess.
Oh?
I think the medication's wearing off.

6 DETENTION

The guard comes in and offers us a cigarette; we mutely reject the all-too-obvious ploy. After that he never offers us another thing. For our part, we now plead constantly for cigarettes, but it does no good. Not that it matters: neither of us smokes, we just do it for something to do. Frequently we are made to pose in women's underwear, or are chained to each other for hours, naked, in an unyielding embrace. These are the moments for which we live. If it ever occurs to them that Sabu and I are lovers, their revenge, I am sure, will not be pretty. Fortunately, they are homophobic blockheads, for whom acknowledging that one man might desire another is tantamount to self-annihilation. These crew-cut frat boys, fresh from squeezing the teats of the high school prom queen, are all rigidity and vacuity; they get to the desert and their exoskeletons collapse. All that's left to them is fear and power, and a sea of interchangeables like me and Sabu, ready to drink their blood at the first sign of weakness. This is the sheerest nonsense, of course, though it is true that, in the long hours alone in the darkened cells, we take turns slowly shaping our teeth to points with a fingernail file we took from one of their fallen comrades. It doesn't mean anything; we just do it to pass the time. I don't even like the taste of their blood.

7 **STORY**

You think you know what you're talking about, but you don't, and you're always the last to find out. What's worse, it only dawns on you when it's too late to do anything about it. For instance, a man walks into his broker's office and demands an immediate accounting. For his part, the broker has already had a difficult day and so, angered by this sudden collapse of confidence, he draws a weapon and beheads his client. Forensic investigation reveals that the head is severed from the spine at an angle of 35 degrees from the horizontal by a single, savage downward blow from a razor-edged blade that comes to rest embedded in the right shoulder of the now-headless corpse. The broker, embarrassed by this *faux pas*, and perhaps even a little put out, leaves his office by a back entrance, saying nothing to his secretary, nor to any of his colleagues; he is apprehended a short time later in a small, dimly-lit bar near his boyhood home where, despite his inebriation, he is arrested and charged with leaving the scene of an accident.

The police are at a loss to explain his return to his old haunts at so inauspicious a time, and so must release him on his own recognizance until the grand jury convenes to hand down its indictment. On his way home, the broker, now without a car for the first time in more years than he cares to remember, is forced to walk through neighborhoods filled with laughing, happy children, and is struck by the proliferation of shaggy-haired family dogs and truck-mounted ice cream vendors moving among them. His suit jacket slung over his left arm, he loosens his tie with his other hand and mops his brow with the handkerchief he has already taken from his jacket pocket. The heat is stifling. Though he would prefer they didn't, he cannot keep his thoughts from wandering back to the beheading; in consternation he kicks a passing dog, only to have it turn and sink its teeth viciously into his leg. Letting out a howl of pain, he stumbles backward and falls clumsily into the street, his head coming to a jarring rest just a few feet from one of the ubiquitous ice cream trucks. Momentarily stunned by the blow to the back of his skull, he doesn't see the truck as, heavily laden with frozen delights, it backs over his head, which explodes like a watermelon dropped from a great height onto a cement floor.

That night his wife, alone in their oversized bed and unaware of what has transpired, ruminates on the strange turns that life sometimes takes and decides that this will be the last time she will sit up waiting for her husband to come home from "work." The next morning she gets up and leaves to make a new life in another city, somewhere far away from the sordid memories that have kept her imprisoned for so long.

8 DEJA VU

They told me I was old and unproductive and they had just the place for me. Then they mentioned the Albigensians – about whom I have no knowledge – and recited to me collectively the Protocols of the Elders of Zion. "Surely these words have long been discredited," I protested, but they continued, undaunted, in sing-songy voices that belied the extremity of their beliefs. At the end of the ceremony I was pitched headlong from the tumbrel and rolled fitfully down the embankment to the river's edge. "Vive la France!" I cried, thankful that this was the extent of my knowledge of that execrable tongue. "Après moi, le déluge!"

9 **FATHERS DAY**

The message from the chief finally got through. His only instruction was: "sit tight." Sit tight? What does that mean? I've never heard of that, sit tight. What if I can't sit tight? What if, in my ignorance, I fail to? What if my energies flag and I end up, despite my best intentions, sitting loose? Then what? Are there consequences? Or is there some indeterminate state somewhere in between, sitting neither loose nor tight? Am I safe there? Or is tight the only kind of sitting that will ensure survival? And shouldn't it be sit *tightly*, anyway? Or is "sit tight" a phrase like "look sharp," which is not so much an admonition to be *looking sharply* as to appear alert and intellectually agile? Though it seems to me it's also used as a way to get others to hurry up, no? My father used to say: "Do so-and-so, and look sharp about it." I dug in my heels, naturally. He was convinced I was dull-witted. I was convinced he was indifferent, if not hostile, to my existence. Ah, the age-old gap, father and son, son and father. If he were alive today I'd have to kill him. Again. Hmm . . . I wonder if my own son entertains such patricidal impulses? I hadn't thought about that one – I'll have to be on my guard. I wouldn't put it past him, the little twerp. But what would he have to gain? Peace of mind? Probably. A general sort of unburdening? No doubt. Inherited wealth? Ha ha. But what about the love and affection, wouldn't he miss that? Not from me, I mean, but from whoever he must be getting it, for surely he must be getting it from someone. But then why would my death deprive him of somebody else's love and affection? And who is the guilty party anyway? His mother? I wouldn't put it past her either. They say that women are more at ease with the emotions. The way they repeat it so incessantly you'd almost think it was a good thing.

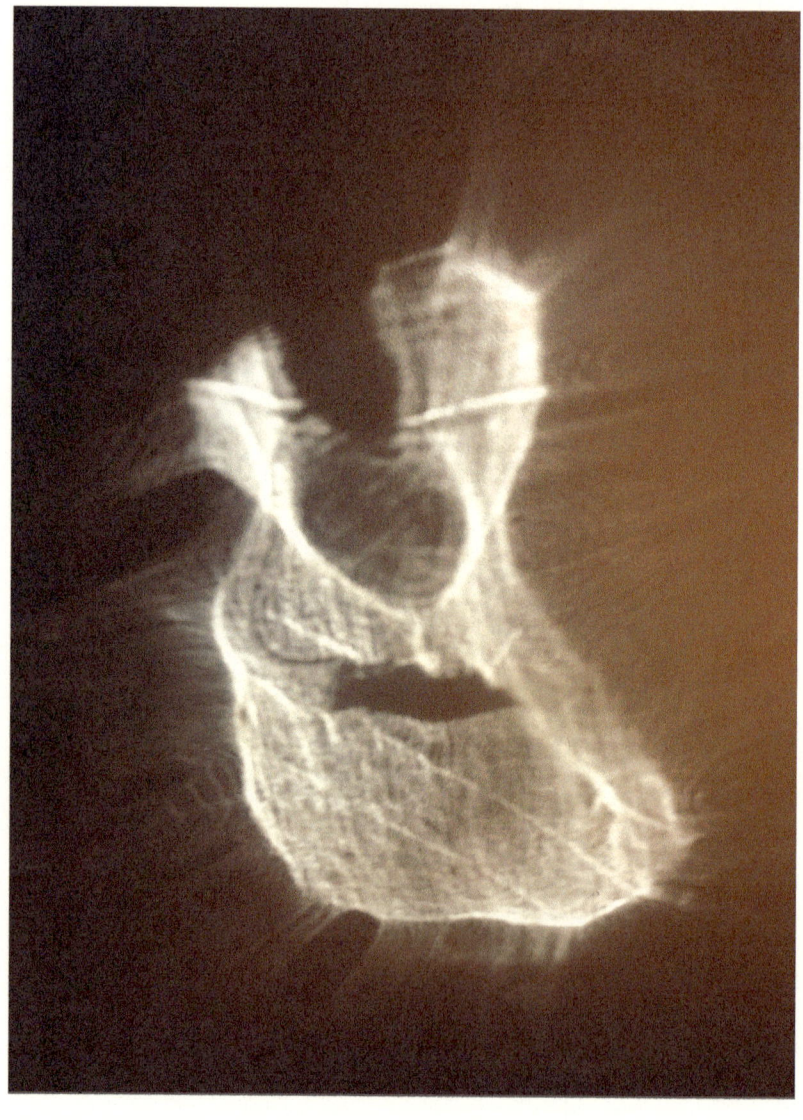

10 THE REPROBATE

It may happen that a man wakes up one day . . . and the rest is history. In a nutshell. The horror, on the other hand, is gone, and in its place, a yawn. After which he dresses, somberly, neglecting, again, to bathe, and descends the staircase to the dining room below. Outside, the rain is unremitting, his temples throb, Atlantis. Oh, for a life on the open road – I could be a yobbo, brandish a stick, kill dogs, frighten small children. I dreamt I was the corner of a building in a neglected part of the city, after which I was apprehended again and again, though always by unknown assailants whose desire, they claimed, was only to "know me better." I cursed them under my breath. They forced me to wear women's clothing. The fools! Nothing could have pleased me more. As a woman I could be trained in the pneumatic and hydraulic arts, I could make a killing in the stock markets. Once I could even strangle small mammals with my bare hands, but that was before. It's all behind me now. All the little pleasures seem somehow to have lost their sting – have you noticed that? Or is it just me?

Another time I was eaten piecemeal by the ancient gods of the Tlaxcala. They recognized me from the photograph at the post office, in spite of the fact that everyone agreed it was not a good likeness. That, I suppose, is why they are gods and we are not. Just out of curiosity, I asked them, "What sets things in motion?"
"Conflict," said one.
"The unmoved mover," said another.
"Desire," said a third.

"Lack," added a fourth.

"Boredom," said the last, stifling a yawn.

"You call yourselves gods," I snorted, "you wouldn't know the answer if it came up and bit you." Why do I waste my days like this, I thought, when I could be a piling, or a piece of burst inner tube at the bottom of the sea. I could rule the world from a seat by the window if I didn't have to get up to shit and piss.

Later I was expelled from the Garden of Eden for failing to brush my teeth after every meal. "Who put you in charge?" I said as I was leaving. Nobody answered.

11 **LOST LOVE**

Well, alright, I was in love – once. She used to wear flowers in her hair. That was before everyone started doing it. Way ahead of her time she was, a real individual. Not like today. Today, one's doing it, they all gotta do it. Not her though. Someone started doing something she was doing, she'd pound 'em – they'd pretty soon stop. She used to shave her you-know-what – I know, I saw it once. Reminded me of, like, baby mice or something. Don't ask me why. Slapped my hand when I tried to touch it. No, she didn't brook no monkey business when it come to that. She did let me hold her titties once or twice, from in front *and* behind, but her daddy caught me at it one time and he soon put a stop to that. I don't want to speak ill of the dead, but I swear I seen him eyeballin' 'em just the same as me, more'n once – and her his own flesh and blood!

Took a bus once to Jehovah, Montana. Strange name for a town, 'specially one as barren and worthless as what that one was. Thirteen hours on a Greyhound bus. But it was as good a place to go as any other, and I had to go somewhere. Holed up in a motel there as long as I could stand it, finally give it up and come back to face the music. Nobody even noticed I was gone. Meantime they'd already jailed some poor black bastard for it anyway. All that time and money for nothin'.

Still, I guess I did get to see something of the world outside this flea-bit sinkhole – enough to know I didn't want to see no more. So what's that leave? Not here, not there. Too many people nowadays think you gotta always be on your way somewhere. Not me. If you can't be happy where you're at, how you gonna be happy someplace else? Sure wouldn't mind having that old girl back sometime, though, hairless poontang and all. But I ain't picky like I used to be. Used to be I wouldn't let a girl touch me down there, but, you know, things change. Long as she wash her hands, I figure what's the harm? Still ain't gonna let 'em put their mouth on me, though – uh-uh, that just is not happenin'. You know how many germs a mouth's got in it? And what if she gets pissed at you and sets out to bite that thing off? Makes me shiver just thinking about it.

12 **HYSTERY**

In the street I am accosted frequently by gaunt men dressed in rags. It is Prague, or Vienna, the late summer of 1938 or '39. Hitler is not yet in the Sudetenland, or the Rhineland, I forget which. Nonetheless, my days are numbered, as are everyone else's, though few seem to be aware of it, and fewer still inclined to do anything about it.

The gaunt men in rags began appearing in the spring. At first their presence was jarring, but now we flinch only when we come upon them unexpectedly. On the Boulevard today one of them asked me if he could take me out to the ballgame, then winked suggestively. Who knows, perhaps I'll go. I'll ask my parents tonight, though something tells me they won't be receptive. They're very concerned about the fifth column; they think he will try to insert it between my legs. They're convinced I'm sex-obsessed because I collapse in a froth when the dirigibles pass overhead. I tell them it's not about the sex, but they just scoff at my naivete.

My father insists upon walking with me through the Casbah to school each morning. He says all those Arab boys are worse than the Italians – they can smell sex on the air, he says, and they breed like rabbits. He also says we have enemies everywhere. He never specifies who the enemies are, but then it's never really clear who is included in the *we*, either. Sometimes I think he only says *we* for fear of seeming paranoid, or megalomaniacal. He is very conscious of what other people think of him, though I think he would sooner die than admit it.

I have been seeing Herr Doktor Freud for weeks now, all to no avail. He insists we can make no progress until I confront honestly my repressed desires for him and men like him. Poor man! How can I tell him that, between the cigars and the prosthesis, he has the foulest breath imaginable?

People have taken to describing the gaunt men (and now women) as "hollow-eyed" – mother says they look "haunted," but then mother often looks haunted herself nowadays, though not by the spectre of communism, which looks to be, as the Americans say, "dead in the water." Well, that's what she gets for putting all her hopes into yet another dreary statist solution. She, too, is bored senseless with this hopelessly bourgeois existence – why can't she just admit it?

I have stopped seeing Herr Doktor Freud, but still he pursues me with demands to know why I have cut him off so abruptly. In an uncharacteristic fit of pique, I told him I would rather suck the penises of all the Arab boys *and* the Italians than spend another moment in the presence of his rank exhalations. In a fit of pique of his own, he told father what I said. Father says he will see me sold into slavery first.

I have been sold into slavery. No date has been set for the wedding – I haven't even met the poor, hapless young man ("a rising star in the Insurance Institute," mother laughably assures me). But just as quickly as the plans were made, they and every other plan have been unmade by the news from the west: the invasion, long-feared, has finally begun. Soon we will all be gaunt and hollow-eyed, and marriage to a ninny (him, not me!) will be the last thing on anybody's mind. Besides, I have made plans of my own: tonight I will meet my beautiful Arab boy, Ismael, at the docks – we leave at first tide for his homeland in Palestine. He dreams of a new utopia there where people like the two of us can live together in peace, away from this madness. How I do so wish for it with all my heart.

13 AND THIS ONE FROM A YOUNG MAN AT THE FRONT

Gunner's Mate Frantic reporting for duty, sir. Here on Heartbreak Hill we've been waiting for orders to evacuate and all we get is foil-wrapped packages of stale bread and tins of oysters we can't open. I mean, not that we can't open, but we got orders not to. Every night we circle the perimeter with Studebakers and shell-shocked tracking dogs, but the enemy is smart, sir, smarter than we are. Whenever we get there she's gone, and if she's not, we can't tell the difference. Comes the morning and the sky's still a vacant blue and nobody knows what to do next. Hatpin calls in to headquarters at 0-eight hundred like always, but the world's air is filled with static and by then we've pretty much lost interest anyway, so it almost doesn't matter that nobody from CentCom ever answers.

Anyway, what I wanted to say, sir, some of the men have been seeing you in their dreams lately, comin' over the hill with a haystack in every hand, and what we want to know, sir, is where does the truth lie?

Well, the short answer is, anywhere she wants to son, anywhere she wants to. And isn't that just like a woman? Ha ha. But, joking aside, that's a paradox I'm not authorized to untangle, at least not for an enlisted man. I want you to know, though, that everybody back stateside is pleased as punch with the sacrifices you men are making, and whether you die or not, you'll always have the thanks of a grateful nation to come home to, if nothing else.

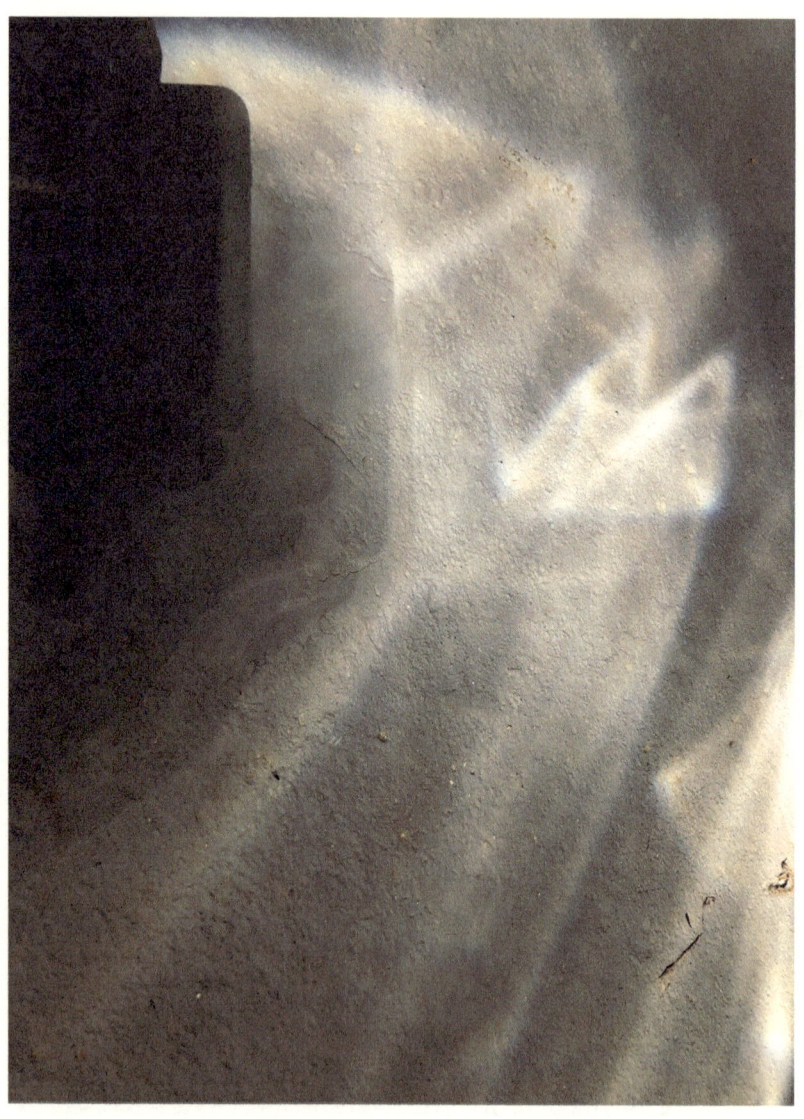

14 DIALOGUE II

When I was discharged they told me the problem was that I was *durable* but not *resilient*.
Did they explain to you what that meant?
They said I had worn well, but I didn't appear to be bouncing back.
Bouncing back from what?
They didn't say.
And so they discharged you?
Yes.
And where were you discharged from?
It's difficult to say – either the military or a mental institution.
Do you know the difference?
Come again?
Do you know the difference?
Between what and what?
Between the military and a mental institution.
Oh, yes: in one they make you wear a uniform.
Do you recall which one?
Which uniform?
Which institution – which institution requires you to wear a uniform.
No.
What did you do when they told you you were to be discharged?
I said, "You can't do this to me, I'm the President!"
You were President at the time?
Or so I thought. They seemed not to credit my claim. Inevitably I began to question it myself.

Inevitably?
You don't think it was inevitable?
I merely raised the question.
You have never suffered the steady erosion of the spirit.
Perhaps, perhaps not – but it is *identity* we are here concerned with, not the spirit.
Are they so easily separable?
So you came to conclude that you were no longer President?
That perhaps I had never even been President.
Is it so important to be President?
Not in itself – I'm not much for honorifics – it's just that, well, if I'm not the President, who am I?
We all ask ourselves that same question from time to time.
You mean, you think *you* are the President also?
No, I mean we – the staff here – ask ourselves, if he's not the President, then who is he?
And your conclusion?
Well, while it would be going too far to say you are intelligent, you are not without a certain native shrewdness. Your shallow affective life is masked by your skill at anticipating what others wish to hear, then tailoring your self-presentation to their desires. Curiously, in your inability to determine where you end and other people begin, you exhibit symptoms of the narcissism so prevalent in 21st century consumer society, while your simultaneous desires to both dominate and be dominated are the sadomasochistic components of a more archaic authoritarian personality type. In observing you, I have been reminded of nothing so much as a quote from Albert Speer, Adolf Hitler's architect and munitions minister, to the effect that, when surrounded by Hitler and his cohort, he could not shake the suspicion that they were all – himself included – little more than a pack of bullying schoolboys masquerading as great men. While he himself did not seem able to make the larger connection, I think this insight could easily be extended to include all such "great" men, even those supposedly genuine ones they thought they were impersonating. After all, I think you'll agree that great men are only great insofar as millions of others are willing to embrace their own diminution, no? So, yes, you could indeed be the President, of this or any country.
Hmm, yes, I see what you're saying. It's not really conclusive,

though, is it? Well, if it helps at all, I do recall another difference.
Between?
The military and the mental institution.
Yes?
In the one you are sometimes required to roll a fragmentation grenade into your officers' tent, whereas in the other there is generally a strict prohibition on the issuance of munitions to the inmates.
But you still don't recall which is which?
No. Should I?
Perhaps not.

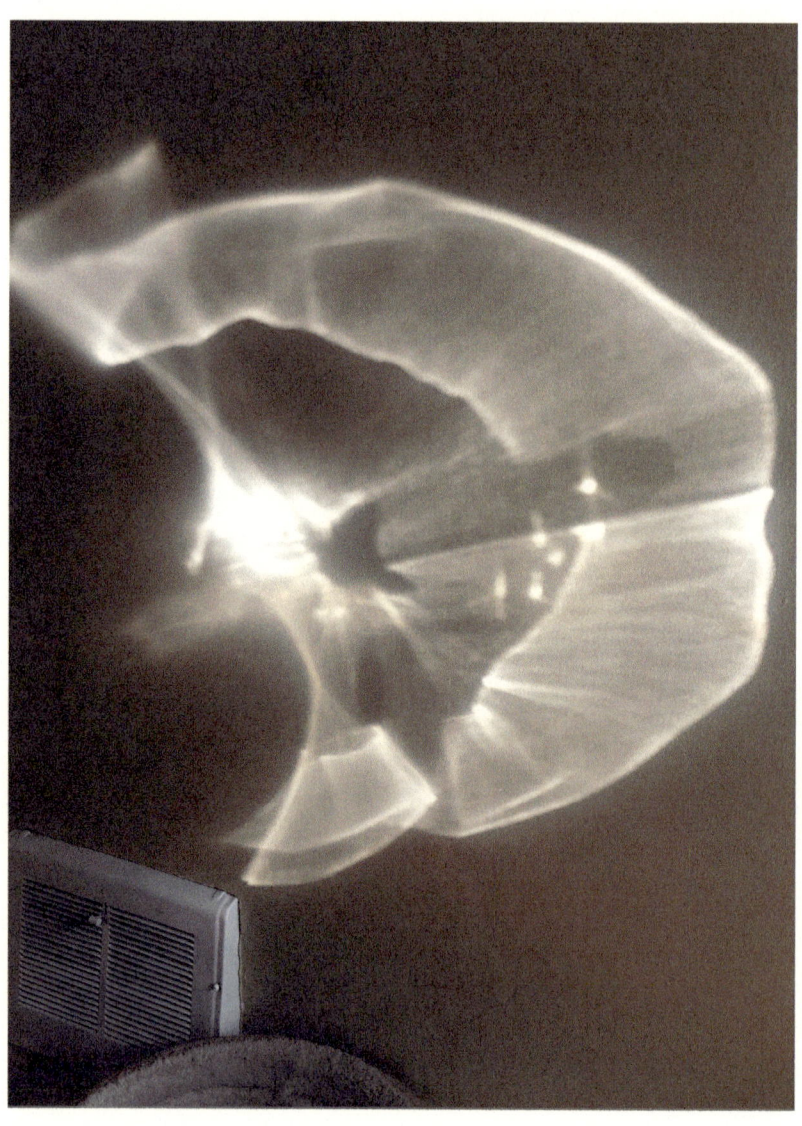

15 HOME IS WHERE THE HEARTH IS

During that time we lived on a blasted heath. When called upon to do so, though, we were more likely to refer to it as *the* blasted heath, or even *that* blasted heath. And when I say we, I mean only that there was more than one of us, though, to be sure, the number was far from large, or stable.

The visible signs of blastedness, I suppose, were typical enough: windswept barrens, limbless trees, lifeless limbs, howling winds, baying hounds, etc. In truth, everything about it was blasted: the blasted cliffs and quarries; the shattered boulders; the stunted shrubs shorn of all but the most tenacious greenery – mostly brownery by then; the humble, blasted little homes of the humble, blasted little people who insisted on dwelling there, if dwelling it could be called; the lofty crags with their silent, weather-beaten fjords – even the office buildings were blasted, or would have been, had nature been allowed to run her course and had she thought, in her wisdom, to provide any. But by then it would probably have ceased to be a heath, I suppose, blasted or otherwise.

Still, there was the broad, flat expanse, stretching, in our imaginations at least, to the mist-shrouded horizon. Except, of course, for those areas where it was neither broad nor flat, but instead ascended abruptly like a series of basaltic steps on the stairway to heaven or, conversely, descended in a headlong tumble down to the heart of the gravitational – though invariably you'd end up colliding with something substantial well before you got there and that was the end of that.

Did I mention the fog? Of course there was fog, it wouldn't have been a heath without fog, or the pervasive dampness, the two seem to go hand in hand, I don't know why. One thing I was never able to clear up was the question of just who or what had blasted the heath. One must assume, I suppose, God, but what if one's belief system doesn't extend that far? What if one has no belief system? Is that a shortcoming or an advantage? Is it even possible?

Naturally, all hell would frequently break loose, weatherwise, which inevitably contributed to the sense of blastedness we all shared. Oh yes, we were all blasted ourselves, how could it be otherwise? You live on a blasted heath, why would you be exempt? But that's the trouble nowadays, isn't it? Everybody's got to be special, everyone the exception to the rule. Whatever happened to satisfaction with one's meager or paltry lot? Was that just a myth? Have I simply been deluding myself all this time, thinking things were better before the invention of the steam whistle, say, or the nation state? As usual, I am the last to know. Is it asking too much to have someone fill me in from time to time? I, who threaten no one?

What's wrong with people today? Am I the only one who notices it, this creeping sense of . . . of what? Of *nomenclature?* What is that? Was I thinking of *nomenklatura?* Well, clearly neither one of them is the word I'm looking for, but I can't for the life of me think of the one that is. Was I thinking of *entitlement?* That's what I hate about this whole aging process, the organ failure. Still, as the wags around the water cooler say, it beats the alternative. Easy for them to say, they don't have to work for a living. But there has to be more to life than retirement benefits, eh? Not that I have any. Not that I would take them if they were offered. Not that anybody's likely to offer them, since I've nothing to retire from. But it's the principle of the thing.

No, it's all or nothing at all for me. Ask my peers, they'll tell you, no half measures for him. Though sometimes I wish there were. Half measures, I mean. It would be a relief, I'll admit, just once to vacillate or equivocate, perhaps even to hem or haw. Life isn't all black or white, they say. Who could disagree, for God's sake? Talk about stating the obvious. Sometimes, you just want to say, do you ever shut up? Or think before you speak?

Not that I am overburdened with excessive self-reflection myself, thank God. You need only look around you a moment to see where thinking has gotten us. This is why, in my heart of hearts, I have always celebrated men of action, men like Winston Churchill or Adolf Hitler. Outside my heart of hearts it's another matter. Outside my heart of hearts, what I've generally celebrated is women who will take their clothes off at the drop of a hat and not thereafter insist that I get a job or a haircut. Do I ask too much? I would not have thought so, but you'd be surprised. The vehemence, sometimes it's just beyond belief. Where were these people brought up? Some of those things I wouldn't say to my worst enemy. Where does all that anger come from? Sometimes I wonder if they even know themselves. If they themselves know, I mean. Though perhaps it makes just as much sense either way. Know thyself, the bible says. Or is it know thine enemy? Aren't they the same thing?

But why, I ask, was I never warned? About the rage I mean. Well, I wasn't going to say anything, but I hold my mother responsible on that score – after all, who better situated to know the sources of female despair? Though, in fairness, my father must have seen his share – couldn't he have said something? Perhaps he wanted to spare me. But spare me what? He didn't seem to care about sparing me much else. Spare me the rod, this much he did do, for he always used his hand. Though in his defense I will say he didn't seem to enjoy it as much as he could have. Not everybody is a natural born sadist, thank God. I count it part of my revenge that I came out of it a spoiled child nonetheless, though perhaps not in the sense that the adage would have it. Though how I'd know the sense in which the adage would have it I've no idea. It's not as if it comes with an explanatory note. Is it general agreement, is that it? Some sort of unspoken consensus? Group delusion? Is adage even the right word?

He himself was not immune to outbursts of stuttering rage – my father, that is. Once, when I was a child, he called my mother a mealy-mouthed bitch – even I could tell it was not a term of endearment. But what exactly did he mean? She, of course, refused to rise to the bait. Who could blame her? He had the upper hand.

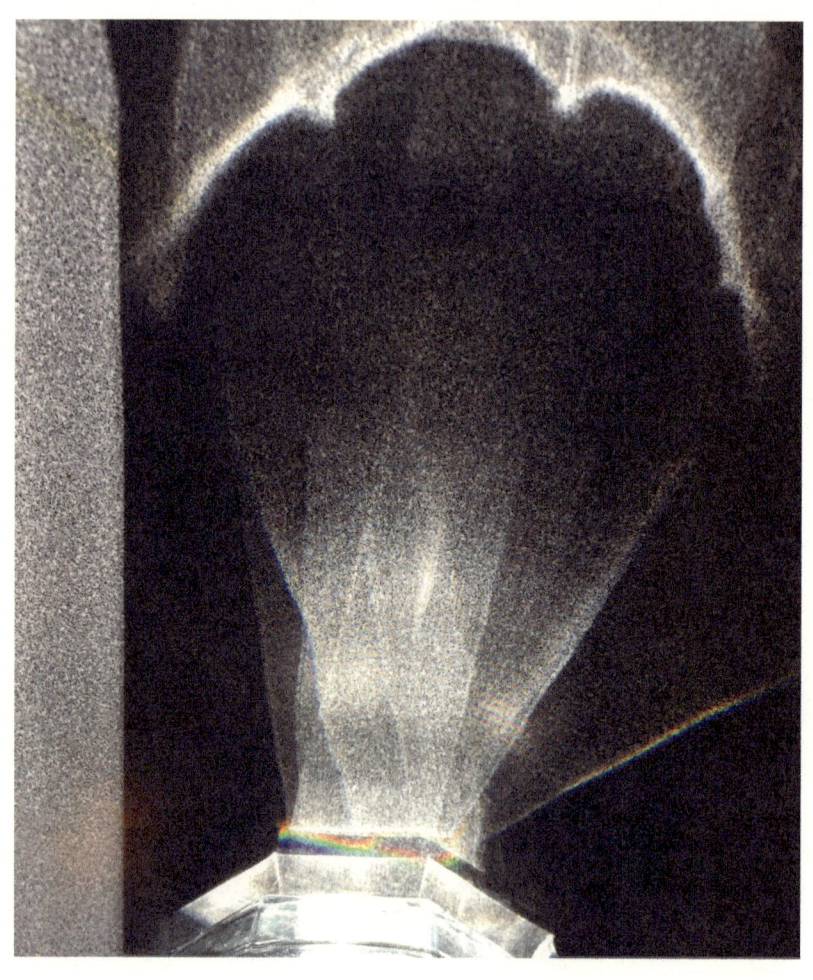

I would have liked it if she'd said, what does that mean, mealy-mouthed? But she didn't, she just sobbed quietly. In my mind I have an image of her wringing her hands, or wringing something in her hands, a handkerchief or a washcloth, but it's probably just a half-remembered scene from some movie, like so much of what I take to be memories of my childhood.

No, we didn't always live on a blasted heath, cut off from humanity and all technological innovation; eventually, like others, we watched motion pictures, we listened to sound recordings, we clustered around the radio dial and later the TV. But that was all much later, after we had left. In fact, that's why we left, why everybody left, eventually: on the rare occasion some stray device would fall into our hands, the reception was uniformly terrible. We put up with it for as long as we could, but after a while you can't help but ask yourself, why the sacrifice? Why the self-denial? Don't we deserve the best like everyone else? It's one thing to live on a blasted heath when that's all there is, but nowadays there's no excuse for not bettering your lot. So, yes, eventually I had a normal upbringing, as normal as anyone's I suppose, full of electronic gadgetry and purposeless rage, estranged from nature as well as my fellow humans – but that's another story.

16 FAME AND FORTUNE

When I finally became a star people flocked from far and wide to worship at my feet. It's a dirty job, they said, but someone's got to do it. I warned you, said my father, don't come crying to me. All my friends abandoned me, naturally; some out of righteous indignation, some out of envy. Still, everywhere I went I was honored and adored. People came to me to bless their newborn children, or to grant them better luck in the next life. Soon I became dizzy and disoriented. Imagine if they'd made you God, said my mother. I'd be happy to see him get a job, said my father. He never understood me, but then I never understood him. What was there to understand? He was a man like any other: squat, sedulous and refractory. And there was I: squat, sedulous and refractory also. But younger.

Needless to say, once the novelty wore off, the adoration rapidly paled to disappointment; not long after that it became resentment, and, finally, of course, rage. I began to suffer blackouts and flashbacks, as well as vertigo and chronic indecision – or is it indecisiveness? They blamed me for all their shortcomings, every failure to thrive, every missed opportunity, every downward turn of their fortunes. I accepted their enmity with equanimity, if only because the two words sounded so much alike. Soon there were death threats, close calls, near misses. Why do we so often like to list things in threes, I wonder? Interestingly, even as my fame was being eclipsed, my already large entourage continued to swell to gigantic proportions. Most of them I didn't know from Adam, but I knew they had my best interests at heart. To be surrounded by so much love, it was unnerving. And expensive. Who's going to pay all these bills? said my father. We'll write them off, said my agent. Who's he? said my father. My agent, I said. Your agent?! he replied; you haven't got a job but you've got an agent? That's how it works, Dad, I said; come on, get with the program. As he left he accidentally shut the door on my hand.

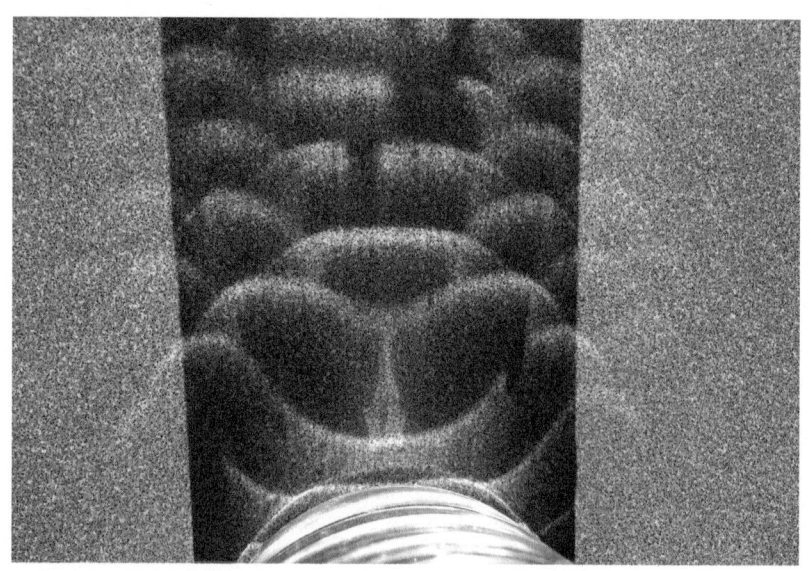

17 STANDOFFISHNESS

It was not a bad life, as lives go. My one goal was to be unencumbered. Unencumbered?! said my father, What kind of goal is that? Where are the grand plans, the empire-building, the vaulting ambition? Your guess is as good as mine, I said – I thought all that was your responsibility. You know your problem, don't you? he continued. You lack gumption; gumption and ambition. And sticktoitiveness. And whose fault is that? I replied. Your mother's, he said. For a long time I thought gumption was something you put on your football boots to keep the water out. When I found out what it really meant his words took on an added poignancy. But by then we were fully estranged: all my letters came back unopened and unread. Then again, I always sent his back unopened and unread also. Why we couldn't have just spoken to each other as we passed on the landing, or sat together before the television set, I've no idea. Perhaps it was a Mexican standoff, though I'm not sure in what way a Mexican standoff differs from other kinds of standoff. It's also true that neither of us was Mexican, though it might have been better if we were: if nothing else I know I've never heard a Mexican child chastised for lack of gumption. Perhaps they have no word for it. They're not like the Germans, the Mexicans; they may not have a word for everything, but at least you can enjoy listening to them speak. The language of love some call it, "la lengua del amor," though I'm told it also translates to the tongue of love, which does take a little of the shine off it from my perspective.

18 NOTHING VENTURED, NOTHING LOST

I was on a park bench, sleeping. All around were small children, silent, eyeing me conspiratorially. It was early morning and I was covered with newspapers. Freedom demands its price, like all things. I say that not because I'm a philosopher, but because I'm an economist. Or was. I had to give it up, like much else, once I'd thought it through. Still, I had my standards: warm as it was, I was not about to sleep naked where the children might see me; who knows the damage it might have done. Hence the newspapers. One of the larger of them – the children, I mean – was quietly urging another, smaller one to set them afire – the newspapers, that is – was even pressing on him the use of his cigarette lighter, despite the fact he could just as easily have done it himself. Oh, yes, he was anxious to see it done, but he didn't want to do it alone; he wanted a collaborator, a co-conspirator. It's touching, really, isn't it, this ceaseless reaching out to others, this unstoppable urge to share? Even if all that's being shared is criminal culpability. But isn't this precisely what makes us human, after all? That and the opposable thumb. And upright bipedal walking. And language, too, improbably enough, as well as an unnaturally large brain. Consciousness also, I would think. And the sanction of the Almighty, some say. I wonder: would a judge have looked more benignly on their misstep then if he saw them merely as two playful scallywags sharing a lark, rather than a pair of youthful sociopaths-in-the-making bent on doing gratuitous bodily harm to a complete stranger down on his luck? Who knows? Who cares, really; even had he ordered them publicly hanged, little good it would have done me in the grave, or encased in bandages and burn ointment from head to toe, another nameless victim of profitless arson.

I threw off the newspapers. That set them back on their little heels I can tell you. I seized the smaller one by the throat and throttled him until his eyes bulged out. Oh yes, I still had it in me. I'd like to say the other one stood glued to the spot, transfixed by terror, but he didn't; he simply withdrew a fist-sized stone, smooth and round, from his trousers pocket, and hurled it full-force at my unsuspecting topknot. Would it surprise you to learn they were gone by the time I came to? Give them their due, though: it was clear they'd done their level best to complete their mission before absconding, but the newspapers, still damp from the urine, had done little more than smolder fitfully. One more day of life! Oh well, you can't have everything. Still, you have to feel for them – all that effort for nothing! No wonder young people today are reluctant to take on anything more demanding than a career.

19 **YES, BUT WHAT ARE YOU FEELING?**

They wanted to know what I was feeling. Feeling? I said. Why, nothing. I try to feel as little as possible, generally. Just to keep things simple. Not out of any aversion to emotional entanglement, though; oh, no, I can entangle with the best of them, if that's what's called for. I'm nothing if not adaptable, even if adaptability sometimes calls, paradoxically, for a rigid inflexibility – and I am not here speaking just about my penis, which is itself nothing if not flexible, even when rigid.

I recall reading in an issue of the National Geographic Magazine once of the search for a minor subspecies of great ape which was said to have evolved a prehensile penis. Had they thought to ask me I could have saved them a lot of unnecessary travel in this regard, but then, isn't unnecessary travel largely what the magazine is about? Though who am I to say; as far as I'm concerned all travel is unnecessary travel. Get out and see the world, my father said the first time he pushed me out the door. The wind howled remorselessly about my ears. But father, I'm only three, I shouted at the top of my little lungs. Stop making excuses, he shouted back through the closed and locked door, you'll never get on in the world if you keep avoiding challenges. Personally I think he would have been happy if I never made it beyond the shed at the end of the garden, as long as I at least made it that far. I think the idea of fatherhood appealed to him in the abstract – he was a great one for brief, volcanic enthusiasms – but the reality of a snotty, pukey, crap-laden, drooling dependent soon cured him of any lingering illusions he harbored on that score. Later he would tell anyone who would listen that, though he may well have begotten me (he insisted there was no conclusive proof), he was under no obligation to compound the felony by welcoming me into his heart and hearth.

They say Adolf Hitler was also the byproduct of ambivalent parenting; I could hardly expect to be alone in my travails, I suppose. Is it true that he was toilet-trained with a whistle and a sharp stick? Who can say, but if he was, it was certainly not at the hands of his besotted mother, who doted on him just as if he were a real human child. And, as if ordinary family dynamics weren't difficult enough, he was dogged throughout his life by rumors that he was his own mother's half-brother! That is, that his father and his mother's father were one and the same person! Who wouldn't want to annihilate *somebody* after that?

20 MINE EYES HAVE SEEN THE GLORY OF HIS TERRIBLE SWIFT SWORD

I have not had much truck with religion in my life. My parents warned against it; they said it would cause atrophy. I tried it anyway. It was easy enough to find, most of the world suffers with it. Curiously, those who are most afflicted seem the most eager to share their affliction. It is said that misery loves company, and it is true, for it's the sharing I miss most. Sharing the tall tales; sharing the host; sharing your woes, burdens, miseries; sharing your meager earnings with the parasite who runs the place. Omlet was his name – strange name for a priest, if that indeed is what he was. Strange name for anyone if you think about it, but there it is. Father Omlet. Mullah Omlet. Vicar Omlet. Rabbi Omlet. The Right Reverend Sir George Omlet. Who knows? But he was not all bad. The parishioners loved him, in their own inimical little parishioner way. Did I say inimical? I meant inimitable. And heaven knows they took his pronouncements seriously enough, which is more than they ever did for me. Mine. I hold no grudges, though; I'm bigger than that. If they think his heavenly mumbo-jumbo will serve them better in the long run than mine, let them have it, I say. I mean, it's the way of the world, isn't it? The prophet is always without honor in his own land. Or her. Not that this is my own land; no, far from it. Which may have been part of why they resented me so much – people make such a fuss about origins and tribal affiliations and what have you. I would've thought my supposedly "exotic" appearance would be part of my charm, but in the exit polls most of the ones who did turn up said they found it "distressing," and my presence among them "deeply disturbing." Why that should be I've no idea, for one of the things I've always prized in myself is my ability to fit in. Never a word of complaint from me, no. No backtalk, no second-guessing the lads in charge, just yes sir, yes sir, three bags full, my little cloth cap balled up in my quivering little squirrel hands, eyes averted, face downcast, the perfect picture of simpering acquiescence. What a sight I must have been. Many's the time I would've been tempted to hit me myself, had I been one of them. The enemy, I mean.

21 THE JOB

They took me out to the stonecutter's yard and showed me a pile of dirt as big as a small house.
"This needs to be moved from here to there," they said, pointing to the far end of the yard. One of them handed me a shovel.
"Do well today," he said, "and tomorrow we'll give you a wheel barrel."
"An incentive like that," I said, "what could hold a man back?"
"Enough of your backchat," said the other, "get on with it."
By the end of the day I was sweating like a pig and had barely made a dent in the pile. They approached me obliquely, from the back of the row houses, and expressed their disappointment with my output.
"The quality of your work is beyond reproach," said the one, "it's the quantity that leaves something to be desired."
"But knowing how much you wish to make a good first impression," said the other, "we're willing to make an exception this time and let you keep the shovel, rent free, and work through the night." I thanked them for their generosity but insisted it wasn't necessary. They insisted it was.
It was a moonless, starless night, and though I was at my best in the cool and quiet, the later it got the harder it became for me to see. The yard being littered with rubbish and bits of disused stone, much of my time was spent stumbling into things, crying out in pain, and dropping the shovel. Towards morning I fell in a hole.
When I came to, the sun was up and I was startled to

discover the two of them standing over the hole and gazing off in consternation at the end of the yard. I peered over the edge in the direction they were staring: there stood the original pile, seeming untouched, in all its pristine glory.

"What do you suppose happened to the new pile," said the one.

"It's as if there never was one," said the other.

Slowly it dawned on me. At some point early in the game I must've gotten turned around, and thereafter spent the rest of the night carrying the little bit I'd moved during the day back to the original pile. I sank back into the hole and steeled myself for the inevitable recriminations.

"Don't think twice about it," said the first as he looked down, "it could have happened to anyone."

"Don't even give it a second thought," said the other. "As long as you're alright, that's our only concern." I was lost for words. This is what happens when you stop looking for the good in people, I thought to myself. They even said I could stay in the hole and rest more if I wished to, so moved were they by my diligence, and insisted on putting sheets of newspaper over my head to keep the sun out of my eyes while I slept. Moved in turn by their tenderness, I rolled over and went back to sleep.

When next I awoke the sun was high in the sky and I was surprised to hear the sound of their voices instructing a new man in the niceties of the task at hand.

"This needs to be moved from here to there," said the one, handing him a shovel and pointing to the other end of the yard, "but first, take some dirt and fill in this hole."

"Do a good job today," said the other, "and tomorrow we'll see about a wheel barrel."

"Don't listen to them," I whispered from beneath the newspaper, "it's not wheel barrel, it's *wheelbarrow.*"

22 STAKHANOV IN THE 21st CENTURY

They told me I was guilty of incredible presumption. You'll have a very hard time finding presumption more credible than mine, I said; I've won awards for the credibility of my presumption. We're not happy with the level of your dishevelment, either, they said, changing the subject. They apologized for the internal rhyme and went on. You could be doing a better job, they said. Sooner or later they always say that. But where do they get this idea? What makes them think I'm some kind of reluctant genius? If I could do a better job, don't they think I'd be doing it? Well, that's not true, either. I know better than to do a good job. Do a good job and the next thing you know they're calling you an invaluable employee and tucking you into bed at night with a kiss. That's how they came to give me the alarm clock – as a reward, they said, for a job well done. What, I said, no thumbscrews? They pretended not to hear me. I threw the alarm clock down the stairs that night when I was alone in the hovel, then I smashed the broken pieces with a hammer and jumped up and down on the mechanism, which had been advertised to me as genuine Swiss-made but clearly bore the legend "Hong Kong" inflicted on its cheap metal casing. It was an empty gesture: despite my best efforts, I still found myself getting to work on time, even without it. In desperation I started drinking myself into a stupor every night, but still I woke with the sun as if I hadn't a care in the world. When I began drinking myself into a stupor during the day they complimented me on the improvement in my morale and made me supervisor of the entire enterprise. I torched the building that same afternoon, with the bosses and all the other employees inside it. I didn't want to, but I knew if I let them live they'd just end up rising, Phoenix-like, from the ashes, the way humans do, and start the whole melancholy process all over again.

Well, the wheels of justice grind exceeding slow, but never let it be said they don't grind at all. I sat back to await my comeuppance at the hands of the law, and sure enough I eventually received a visit from two strapping lads presenting themselves as Sergeant Goiter and Inspector Nelly. To my surprise, they warmly congratulated me on being the only survivor of the cataclysm and informed me that, as such, I had not only been granted a lifetime position as CEO by the owners, but had been put in sole charge of restoring the charred and gutted ruins to their previous glory.

Good Christ, I said, is there no peace? though why I thought there should be I can't begin to imagine. We get no peace, they said, why should you? What could I say? Their logic was impeccable – I might even say irrefutable if I could be sure I was using the word properly. But really, when all's said and done, isn't that precisely what unites us in time of need, that enduring willingness to share with each other everything we have? Even if it's only misery.

23 DIALOGUE III

Do you know how you come to be here?
I think because I didn't follow orders?
Why didn't you follow orders?
Well, uh . . .
You were ordered to follow orders, were you not?
Well, yes, I suppose so . . .
You suppose so? Were you or were you not?
Yes.
Yes what? Yes you were ordered to follow orders, or yes you were not?
Yes.
You are not being very cooperative my friend.
Look, I know things don't look so good for me right now, but I'm trying to, like, think positive here. I'm tired of saying no.
You're tired of saying no?
Yes. I want to look on the bright side, you know, like, sunny side up.
Sunny side up – what does this mean?
It means, like, the glass is half full.
Glass? What glass?
Like, there's a glass with wine in it to the halfway mark – some people say it's half full, some people say it's half empty.
And so? Where is this glass? Whose glass is it? Is it your glass?
It's not anybody's glass, it's just a way of looking at things. If you say the glass is half full you're, like, sticking to the bright side, you're not giving in to despair.

Despair? Most people despair when they have no wine – why would you despair with half a glass?

Some people are just built that way, I guess; they're always looking on the dark side.

Are you one of those people?

I'm trying not to be – I'm trying to be thankful for what I've got.

And what have you got? A glass half full of wine?

I've got the sun in the morning and the moon at night.

These are your personal possessions?

The world belongs to everyone. The best things in life are free.

Oh, you mean like food, shelter, clothing – those free things?

No, I mean, like, even if I don't have any material goods, I've got life, and the natural world, and God's bounty.

How will you know, if we put you in a dark, windowless cell and leave you there?

Well, I just don't want to give in to despair is all.

Perhaps you should. Perhaps it would do you good to see what it is like. Tell me, have you ever had the misfortune to be tortured?

Heck, no – I'm an American.

Americans are not tortured?

Well, I should hope not.

Do you trust that we will not torture you?

Well, why would you?

Perhaps our glass is half empty. Perhaps we've already given in to despair. Perhaps we just enjoy seeing other people suffer. Or perhaps we hate you and everything you stand for.

I don't stand for anything, I'm just me.

You Americans, you have such a way with words.

Well, thanks.

It wasn't meant as praise. Tell me, have you ever wondered what it would be like if you did give yourself over someday to, say, despair, or rage, or hatred?

My guess is, bad things happen when you do that.

24 **HERE COMES THE SON**

Alright, so perhaps I have been a little harsh in my judgement; perhaps the world isn't such a bad place after all. Why, only yesterday the clouds at last lifted, the sun broke through, and birds once again twittered joyfully in the trees outside my window. I even resisted the urge to shoot them. At first. Now the animal cruelty people are hounding me for "donations." It's that or prosecution, they insist. They insist! What is the world coming to? My father, having shot the birds, would simply have shot the animal cruelty people as well then gone back to his butchering and not thought twice about it – and here I sit writing an impotent screed! They don't make them like that anymore. Thank God.

Yes, he was a butcher, my father – chops, steaks, flanks, loins, the lot. I could have done it myself, but I didn't have it in me. It's difficult enough as it is to eat the things without first having to kill them and chop them into unrecognizable pieces. And that smell, it never really leaves you, does it? Even in death he reeked of dead animals. Though, to be fair, being a dead animal himself at the time, some of that was only to be expected.

So, yes, he was a butcher – a pork butcher, to be exact. Why he would not butcher other animals I have no idea, he wouldn't talk about it. In fact, there was very little he would talk about. A taciturn man he was, silent and self-contained. Not happy. No, far from it. Close-mouthed, some said; sullen, said others. Others yet described him as withdrawn, not cut from the common cloth. I won't tell you what his mother called him, though she, I suppose, would be in a position to know. But surely his minister or priest would have agreed with these assessments as well, had he been a believer – my father, I mean, not the priest. But he knew one thing. At least he said he did. Would he share with me its secrets? He would not. And that is why I will not share them with my son, fume and bluster as he may. And that is why he keeps me locked up here, in the vain hope that I will divulge. After all, how is a man to make his way in the world if his sire will not divulge? Well, I had to do it, he'll just have to buck up and get on with it. It's not so hard; sooner or later he'll blunder onto something and it'll all make sense, or at least appear to. Perhaps someday, when it's too late to make any difference, I, like my father before me, will confess to my child that the only reason I didn't divulge was because no one divulged to me. Seems only fair.

But to think that this whole chain of non-divulging could stretch back through the mists of time, generation after generation, perhaps even to the origin of the species, or at least to the onset of so-called civilization. A disheartening thought. What things couldn't we have done if we'd known! But known what? Well, who knows, it could have been anything, couldn't it: the secret to happiness, God's shoe size, the square root of negative one. Still, the world, they say, is consolation enough. Oh, really? To whom? For what? Where do these inanities even come from? Did I learn them as a child at my father's knee? Or was it my mother's? What was I doing at their knees anyway? Why would anybody think that a good place to learn? I would have preferred school, but that's only because I lacked the courage or imagination to do otherwise. Plus, they, who had themselves elevated non-mingling to a way of life, adamantly refused to let me mingle with others of my kind anyway. Perhaps it's a good thing to fear your own species, I don't know.

25 GREAT EXPECTATIONS

She wore a hand-printed t-shirt that read: Piss me off and pay the consequences. Fuck me beyond all imagining, I said under my breath. In the morning I was alone again, just like before. Is that what I wanted, or what I feared? I called in sick. The receptionist said my absence would save the company money and I should stay out as long as I wanted. There was an explosion on the dragline that afternoon and my temporary replacement was instantly dismantled by the shockwave that followed – the footage from the security cameras, suppressed by the TV stations, was an immediate and protracted hit on the web. I never saw it, but I felt bad for the guy anyway. In the morning I reported back to work; at first they pretended not to know me, then they admitted that they did but were trying to avoid paying me unemployment benefits while the line was still down. How long will it be down? I said. Weeks, they replied, maybe months. No arguing with that, I said, and headed for the unemployment office with a smile on my lips and a song in my heart. That night I got shitfaced on red wine and a couple of percodans and passed out on the raggedy-ass couch in the living room. Jesus Christ it had been a beautiful day.

26 THE PROBLEM

How deceptive appearances can be! Why, just the other day I was thoroughly beguiled by a charming young woman who turned out to be a man. Such beautiful breasts! And a penis half again as long as my own. Where to begin? Or even end? I asked her/him to put the pyjama bottoms back on and just let me suckle at the breasts, but somehow all the pleasure had gone out of it. I left, crestfallen, my tail between my legs.

Is there nothing left in this world that is natural? As an infant I refused to be circumcised, bawling at the top of my lungs because I knew it to be a mockery of God's creation. Why would we be born into this world with something that immediately required painful corrective trimming? Admittedly, hair, and nails, do eventually require trimming, and, of course, there is the umbilicus, but I don't think they're the same thing; after all, I deeply enjoy my yearly haircut, even though the experts assure me it has more to do with unconscious fantasies of submission than anything else. What do they know? Personally I think circumcision is just an excuse for certain New York *mohels* to trim little baby penises with their teeth, but, of course, I have no proof beyond what I read in the newspapers.

That's the problem with religious fanatics: they never know where to draw the line. The priests at least wait until you've grown up a little before they start rubbing your neck and shoulders and expressing approval of how well you've come to fill out your trousers this year. They say

I missed my calling in not becoming one – a priest, I mean – but, frankly, I hadn't the heart for it, even though by all accounts it beats working by a country mile. I have enough difficulty controlling my urges as it is, without having to make a "lifestyle" of it: that seems to me to be asking for trouble.

27 CIVILIZATION

Well, it's not an easy subject to broach, your lordship. You see, it's my filthy, shit-encrusted bumhole that I'm most concerned about.
How so?
Well, what does it say? I mean, about my habits of personal hygiene?
Nothing good, I would venture to say.
And beyond that, how does it reflect on my state of mind, my mental and emotional well-being?
Well, it is true that people are not drawn to your company.
But surely the Bible teaches us that, in God's eyes, no man is so abject he cannot wipe the shit-crust from his fundament when called upon to do so.
I'm all too well aware, sir.
Well then, for heaven's sake, man, wash it.
That's just it, your lordship: I mean to, I want to, and each day I set out to do it, but for some reason I cannot. Something in me refuses, I cannot explain why: my gorge rises and I am helpless to comply.
Come, come, man – there's nothing mysterious or weighty to the task, I do it myself, daily. You simply take a soapy washcloth and wipe – up or down, it matters not – making sure to rinse thoroughly afterwards in deference to others with whom you may share its use. The washcloth, I mean.
Still your lordship, my heart cries out each time: what is the point?
Point, sir?! Point?! There is no point, unless you think that raising ourselves up from the muck-wallow is point enough in itself! Were you hog-tied as a child?

Bullwhipped? Hamstrung? Frazzled? Was affection withheld? Did needs go unmet? I assure you, as commonplace as these insults to the central nervous system are, none of this will suffice to excuse this most odious of transgressions. Guard! Give this man a hot meal, fresh bed linens and a safe place to sleep—
Why, thank you, my lord—
But first have his anus scoured with a wire brush drenched in gasoline.

28 EMPLOYEE OF THE MONTH

They told him he was a miraculous mover of product. I suppose that's a compliment, said the honoree. They gave him a gold watch and a tin ear. What am I supposed to do with these? he said. Nothing, one of them replied; they're purely symbolic, no intrinsic value whatsoever. Take them in the spirit they're given. Anyway, it's the thought that counts, remember? Here, help yourself to a donut, said another one, leading him to the food table; coffee's on us, too – take as much as you want. The honoree struggled to remember – is it the thought that counts? Or is it only the thought that it's the thought that counts that counts? I don't think Karl Marx would agree with that, he said. Or Jean-Paul Sartre. Agree with what? said the supervisor. That it's the thought that counts, the honoree replied. It's just something people say, for crisesakes, said the super – it doesn't have to mean anything. I mean, said the honoree, a drowning man's not going to thank you for *thinking* about saving him, if that's all you do. Of course not, said the other, but odds are your drowning man will soon end up a *drowned* man, anyway, and then what difference does it make? You want to be a drowned man with him? Remember, he who fights and runs away, lives to fight another day. What's fighting got to do with drowning? said the honoree; you might be able to fight and run away, but you can't drown and run away. Nobody said you could, replied the super, but if you use a little foresight you can avoid besmirching your new wingtips and plan on saving the *next* drowning man you see, providing this time there's no risk involved and he isn't a competitor. I don't have any competitors, said the honoree. Of course you don't, said the other, I'm talking about the company's competitors; nobody's going to compete with you, you've got nothing worth competing for. I've got a gold watch and a tin ear, he said. Not worth a tinker's damn, said the other – I already told you that. The watch doesn't work any better than the tin ear, and the gold plating isn't. You mean I'm not really valued by the company, said the honoree, despite what it says on the Christmas cards? Context, context, said the super; it's all about the context. And the context is this: you produce value for us, we value you; so long as you produce more value than the others, you'll always be our number one asset, don't you ever doubt it. But what if I stop producing value, or start producing less? Then you're out of here like shit off a shovel. We're not running a charity, you know – this is nature, red in tooth and claw; dog eat dog; kill or be killed; every man for himself; the law of the jungle. But we're not in the jungle, said the honoree. And dogs don't eat other dogs. It's a figure of speech, my friend, said the super, like me calling you my friend when clearly you're not. Would I invite you out to dinner with the family and me? I would not. Would I leave you alone for a minute with my lovely wife who, inexplicably, has some kind of a thing for laconic working class types like yourself? I think that question answers itself. No, if you think about it, it's all just little gestures of domination, really – like me calling some employee *young man* when I'm self-evidently many years his junior, or calling women old enough to be my mother *the girls*, then pretending to improve matters by agreeing to call them *the ladies*. In the manual, incidentally, this is called The Degrading Upgrade.

29 **FRIENDSHIP**

His life was a tilt-a-whirl of unpleasant sensations. Call me a tillerman if you must, but everybody's got to have some kind of a moniker. How I got here is not easy to say, nor is how I went from *he* to *me* in the blink of an eye. When he was asked why, though, his eyes would coruscate with vitriol, and spill down the mountainside as if a dam had burst without warning somewhere in the upper reaches.

His days were filled with emptiness, and when they weren't they were filled with tedium and retribution. Why is it nobody warns us of these things? Why is there so much we must end up feeling forlorn about? Not everything went badly for him, try as he might to insist it did. True, other days were filled with nothing at all, but not all of them. Many's the day I passed in sheer delight remembering the good times we had – does he remember, I wonder? The day we burned down the field behind the housing estate? Or shat together beneath a tree at the top of Barn Hill? What is it keeps us ticking on as if the clock was never going to stop? Sheer doggedness if you're a dog, but what if you're a monkey? Monkeyshines?

Life with his wife was a whirligig of unpleasant observations from both sides, hence their shared conviction that they were made for each other. I never knew her personally – intimately, yes, but never personally. Thank god he never found out. Thus the question of children never arose, for there were none. How would their days have been if there were? Why is it the children inherit every psychoneurological ailment you ever bumped into but never develop into bright golden flowers of happiness, even if you're a bright golden flower of happiness yourself? What is one to make of all the inequality in the world today? What is it about our nature that dooms us to so much iniquity?

On the hillsides he could be seen, having been let out to pasture more times than you could count – hence the doggedness. Monkeyshines, if he had any, he kept to himself, as most of us try our best, or worst, to do in public. And why is it we speak ill of his days, but of his nights, nothing? What must his nights have been like? Sleeping, mostly, I'm inclined to think, but what of his dreams? Did he have any dreams to speak of? Were they of the slumbersome sort or the waking? Did he dream ecstatically of flying through the sky without wings, or did he merely fantasize conquering the Apennines with a pair of crampons and little else? Alas, I'll never know, for most of my nights were spent with the Mrs., and, fortunately, I was always able to beg off sharing days with her as I was nights with him. But where was he while she was with me, and vice versa? And what did he and I do on those days when we weren't burning down fields or shitting wherever we saw fit? Curiously, those are the only two things I can clearly recall us doing during our days together, though more than once I seem to recollect him begging off spending the whole day with me in order to provide a modicum of comfort to his beloved. Whether or not his beloved and his wife were one and the same I was never able to establish.

30 MR. HAPPY GO LUCKY

I have decided to be relentlessly upbeat. It won't be easy, I know. I've not been known for my upbeatness in the past, relentless or otherwise. To the contrary, I think most people who know me at all would think of me as an appalling embodiment of relentless negativity. For instance, one disappointed lover called me "a crabbed, pinched, unimaginative little blowhard, loaded to the gunnels with self-loathing," which I thought was a little harsh even as I was taken by its sailorboy jauntiness. Another said I was self-defeating to a fair-thee-well, and a third said she couldn't bear to live any longer with the pervasive gloom and doom – is it my fault the collapse of the ecosphere should come on my watch? One who was being kind called me bleak, but I think she was just trying to find something nice to say before abandoning me entirely. Later she described leaving me as "like stepping into the sunshine after three years of pouring rain."

31 THE NEXT-BEST GENERATION

Yes, I ate a fair bit of chicken that day. It was one of the good days, when I was still in my prime, and the world was still ours to conquer. It was the earliest months of World War I or II – I can never keep them straight – and we had just moved from Trenton to Wilberforce, to be closer to the action. The country was young then, and vast, and getting around it was nothing like it is today: no such thing as "regularly scheduled" anything. The airplane hadn't been invented, and even the steamboat was in its infancy, to say nothing of the gyrocopter and the hovercraft and other similar ground effects machines.

Work was plentiful back then, and long and arduous for those foolish enough to do it; like the war, we avoided it like the plague it was. Instead we idled away our time with long rambles through the pristine woodlands, making up stories and songs, and dropping our drawers every chance we got. We couldn't any of us keep our pants on in those days, not with the recent discovery of universal birth control, and I remember clearly that day how the sun blazed down on us as we ambled back into town, worn out by a long morning's serial lovemaking. A couple of self-styled patriots took potshots at us from the safety of their little church hideaways, but we didn't care: she walked like she'd been riding a horse all day, and I had her underpants in my pocket – and the rich scent of her on my fingertips – as a keepsake.

Though she'd been raised in a Skinner box at the Orgone Institute, she had about her that fresh, unspoiled country girl look so admired by unhinged urbanized hayseeds like me, and few people watching us pass that afternoon would have given even a moment's thought to the possibility that she might be the nymphomaniac local organizer for the American Communist Red Cross Party. Which, of course, she wasn't, not then anyway – there might have been even more communists if she had been! – but how were they to know? Many people like her were, and when the communists finally did take over it was largely because so many otherwise astute citizens had refused to see what was going on right under their noses (wake up and smell the coffee substitute, new comrades!). When later she had me arrested for deviationist heresies (I didn't even know what deviationist heresies were!), she told me that she, too, would cherish forever that wonderful day, but, nonetheless, for the safety and security of the Party Central Committee, she wanted her panties back.

I called her an Indian-giver, a slanderous term derived from an almost willful misunderstanding of the gift-giving practices of native peoples, but who at the time gave much thought to indigenous populations? We were going to build a new world on the backs of working people everywhere, and we had no time for the inflamed sensitivities of vanishing ethnic minorities, especially ones who lacked even the rudimentary imaginative powers needed to see the stupefying potential of the wheel when they had it. No, we had no patience with the world's losers even then; nor, unfortunately, had they with us, as we later discovered to our great dismay when, having had enough, they finally gathered their scattered forces and drove us unceremoniously back across this great continent to the Atlantic. Who could've imagined? Now what do we do? my compatriots demanded to know as we fled for our lives to the east. Relax, relax, I said, as the sun sank into the sea behind us – it's simple: first chance we get to stop for a break we all ask ourselves, what would Jesus do? When the answer comes, we do it.

32 I AM LEGEND
by Grendel A. Neanderthal

They said I was mean-spirited and unkempt. Tell me what that means and I'll tell you if I am, I replied. They think they can lord it over me with their big words. I crushed their heads like walnuts. With one hand. Little use their big words were to them then. I trampled their flowerbeds and scattered their bones in the fields. I suckled at their mammies' teats and had my way with all their domesticates, fish and fowl alike, until I was sated. Oh, I know they'll expect me to pay for the ungulates, but no more – I've had done with that once and for all. Others of their ilk will come after me now, I know, but I don't care, let them come. I am at home in the forests and fields and they are not, it's as simple as that. I have no need of clothes, or shoes, or electricity, and for that they will always fear me, even after I am dead.

It wasn't always like this. Once we lived in harmony, or at least in mutual toleration; now they're everywhere, there is no way to escape them. But what is one to do: as they burgeon, so we decline.

33 DIALOGUE IV

What seems to be the problem?
I'm having a hard time penetrating.
Don't we all wish we could say as much.
Do we?
No, not really.
Why say things you don't mean?
Why not?
It makes communication difficult.
Communication *is* difficult – it doesn't need any help from me.
Well, that's what I'm saying – it makes it *more* difficult.
Impossible, more like.
Is this a good or a bad thing in your opinion?
Well, why bother talking if you're not going to communicate?
Why indeed.
I thought we were here to talk about my problems.
Your problems? What about *my* problems?
You're the therapist, you're not supposed to have problems.
What human being alive doesn't have problems?
Jesus doesn't.
Jesus is neither alive nor a human being.
He lives in my heart.
I don't think that kind of "alive" is what we're talking about.
What other kind is there?
The kind that you and I represent, here, bodily present and animate, in this room.

How do I know you're alive?
If you don't think I'm alive, why are you talking to me?
Perhaps I'm delusional. How do I know *I'm* alive?
By dint of the fact that you can ask the question.
What does that actually mean, "by dint of?"
Because of, as a result of, made possible by.
Then why not just say that?
Why not just grunt and snort?
Huh? I don't get you.
Exactly.
You know, I don't find your approach very therapeutic.
No? Well tell me what therapeutic means and I'll tell you if it is.
Are you serious? You're a *therapist* and you don't know what *therapeutic* means?
Oh my god, you're right! Therapy, therapist, therapeutic! I can't believe I never made the connection! Guess you really do learn something new every day. So, what about my approach makes you say that?
Well, to start with, I don't get the feeling you're very committed to my getting better.
What would be the point?
Of my getting better?
Of my being committed to it.
How will I get better if you're not committed to helping me get there?
Who told you you were going to get better? Was it someone from this office?
Isn't that what we're here for?
Who knows what we're here for. Some people say we're here to praise God. Really? I mean, really? Create all these people just to tell you how great you are, then toss them into the fry cooker – and I mean for*ever* – if they don't? Wouldn't you think as Commander in Chief of a universe *fourteen billion light years across*, with *who knows how many billions of planets* in it, he could afford to have, oh, I don't know, more *compassionate* things on his mind?
Perhaps he's insecure. No one's perfect.
Exactly my point!
Anyway, I don't believe in God.
Well there you go, that's got to be a huge source of internal

conflict right there – how can you believe in Jesus and not believe in God?
I never said I believe in Jesus; I said he lives in my heart.
Wait a minute – You mean *literally*, like a tapeworm or something? In your *heart*?
Yes.
Hmm. Well, here, listen to this: I'm not the pheasant plucker, I'm the pheasant plucker's son; I'm only plucking pheasants till the pleasant phucker comes.
Is that supposed to be funny?
Some people like it. It's not my favorite, but since you're being so honest and forthright with me, I felt an obligation to reciprocate at least a little bit.

34 POETRY IS YOU, PAYING ATTENTION

You think I'm just an ordinary person, but I'm not. I'm a detective. I detect things, all the time. Just now I'm detecting the possible end of the universe in a vast lake of fire. Of course I'm speaking figuratively. But still the end can't be far off – things can't go on like this indefinitely.

This detecting thing is as much curse as blessing. It pays, of course, to be able to detect when others can't, or won't, but inevitably it sets you apart, because 90% or more of what you detect is animosity, or discord, or just outright anguish. And not anguish leavened by hard won wisdom, or the acceptance of inescapable loss, but just the boundless anguish of resentment and self-pity and an unending sense of personal grievance.

But back to the lake of fire. Of course, the great bulk of my everyday detecting reveals nothing nearly so grandiose as the lake of fire. Much of the time it's just a matter of detecting what's going on around me, a task which, despite its apparent obviousness, not many people seem up to. How many of the recently deceased, for instance, owe their sudden unanticipated demise to a simple failure to detect that their workplace colleague harbors, beneath that stolid if off-putting exterior, an implacable psychotic rage? And always the neighbors and surviving co-workers with the same utterly predictable observations: "But he was always so polite and well-behaved, who could have imagined . . . ?" Polite and well-behaved? That should have been the first warning sign! Do people really not understand repression at all?! Jeffrey Dahmer was polite and well-behaved. Ted Bundy. John Wayne Gacy. Who could have imagined? How about anybody who was paying the slightest bit of attention? Why else would I insist on maintaining the greatest possible distance between me and anyone who persists in addressing me as sir? If that isn't homicidal rage seeking its object I don't know what is.

But the lake of fire is very real, despite my earlier assertion that I was speaking figuratively, and despite the fact that I have thus far detected it only in my dreams. Of course, there's never any shortage of apocalyptic visions in times of social collapse like ours, but at the risk of stating the obvious, let me say again that I am not a visionary but a detective. All my training has been in detecting, none at all in envisioning. And, with all due respect, it also should not be necessary for me to point out that, while a dream may be a dream, it is not, strictly speaking, a vision. Because *dreams* are what you have in your sleep; *visions* are for when you're awake, or, at most, in some kind of waking trance.

So, the lake of fire: is it a vision or a dream? I'd say it was more a hallucination than anything else, or maybe even a nightmare. I know those are very different things, but still there are those who say, and with no lack of conviction, that the differences among visions and hallucinations and nightmares are, at this point, more or less imaginary. Still others might say the lake of fire is simply wish fulfillment.

35 I WOULD PREFER NOT TO

They said I was a parasite because there was nothing about work that attracted my attention. I told them it was productivity I couldn't handle – as soon as I had to think in exchange for money the ideas dried up. Whatever I had to do in this life, there seemed to me no point in doing it unless it was useless or valueless – don't ask me why.

I mean, it's not as if I didn't approach my tasks with alacrity in the beginning. It's not as if I didn't appreciate the necessity to earn a living, to make one's way in the world, to take one's place in the pantheon, but every time I had to do something productive, I shrivelled. Not just my penis and testicles, but my whole physical person – my soul, too, if such a thing could be said to exist. And my brain – my brain clouded over, and my thoughts, well, as I said, they dried up, and I couldn't follow a train of thought for love or money. And those that didn't dry up just turned fuzzy and vaporous. What do you think? My coworkers would say. Or, What are your thoughts? Or later, when my vacuousness was becoming too pronounced to ignore, Got any ideas? Don't pressure me, I said.

They complained about the lack of productivity, called it a failure of the imagination. Perhaps they're right. I tried to think up things they'd value or appreciate, original things, things that nobody had thought of before, but nothing came. What about these pages, I said: don't they count for something? Look how many I've written. Written? they said – Pshaw! anybody can *write* – the real question is, how many have you *sold?* Sold? I said. If I'd thought anybody would give me money for them I could never have written them in the first place. One of them muttered something about self-defeat. Unlike you, I said, drawing myself up to my full, commanding height, I am at one with myself, thank you. You're at one with something, he replied, I'll grant you that. Another one said I needed help but I'd come to the wrong place. You came to me, I said. They grew irritable. Yet another, apropos apparently of nothing, said, Happiness is a warm gun, and stabbed me to death with a knife. Well, there you are, I said as I lay there, just as they say, life is full of surprises. Death not least among them, my assailant added.

36 TRUE STORY

"What's this?" she queried, as my tongue beat vainly at the fortress doors of her clenched teeth, "open-mouthed kissing and you're still underage?" "I'm older than you," I silently replied, which seemed to take her by surprise – if only she knew I was near twice her age! Moments before I had glanced distractedly down the front of her dress as she knelt to sweep up the broken glass before me. "Some of these inanimate objects have attained the capacity to move of their own volition," she said to me one day. "And occasionally even to speak," I countered. It didn't take me long to realize what had gone awry. The white stone awning at the hinge point of the parapet would drift from white to pink if you didn't pay proper attention to it. The other colors, meanwhile, kept disengaging from themselves – I saw them moving slyly from place to place – and the birds chattered truncated versions of their songs to keep from falling asleep. Poplar trees breathed in and out as one bird flew by, its second self a staggeringly blue blue. Others whistled past like winged bullets.

37 J.D. SALINGER DISCUSSES ART AND LIFE WITH ST. PETER

Salinger. Aren't you the one who writes about the Glass Menagerie?
No, that's someone else.
What is a glass menagerie, anyway?
Miniature animals made of glass, I guess. At least, that's what I've always thought.
Of what use are glass animals? Can you do anything with them? Eat them, say?
I think they're strictly ornamental – my understanding is, glass is not very digestible, even if you break it into small pieces.
Likely to have sharp edges, eh?
Small pieces of glass? Yes, I think they are.
So why would you write about them?
Small pieces of glass?
No, glass animals, the Glass Menagerie.
I already told you, that's not me. That's another writer.
That's not what it says here; it says Salinger: Glass Menagerie.
No, I think Eugene O'Neill wrote about a glass menagerie in one of his plays, either him or Tennessee Williams, I often confuse the two. Some character had a collection of little glass figurines. I believe at some point in the play they were smashed.
Must have been expensive, don't you think, a new glass menagerie every performance? So what was the point of introducing these little glass figurines only to have them smashed?
I'm not sure I could say, offhand; I've never read the

play. Knowing Williams' writing – I'm pretty sure now it was him and not O'Neill – I expect it had something to do with fragility, with the ease with which beautiful things – with which beauty is crushed in this world.

Do you feel that beauty is easily crushed?

Do you feel that it isn't?

One must be strong in this world. What point beauty if it can't survive, can't endure?

I suppose you're in a better position to answer that than me.

Tell me, do you think this world is essentially a benign place? Or is it, by its nature, hostile to human existence?

Do you mean *deliberately* hostile? Is it out to get us? Just look at the numbers and you know that's not true. And it seems to me we are the ones who exhibit the hostility.

Why do you think this is? Is there something wrong with us that we can get along neither with other species nor with each other?

Oh, much as I could do without most of them, I think people generally get along with each other much better than we realize. We routinely travel for hours sealed like sardines into commercial aircraft and only very occasionally do we erupt into violence en route. Try doing that with a planeload of chimpanzees sometime.

What about with other species, then?

Yes, well, that's a bit of a different story, isn't it? But, hey, you're the guys who told us to be fruitful and multiply and assume dominion over the Earth. Maybe you should be more careful about what you hand out for advice. And to whom.

Well, perhaps that wasn't our best decision. But who knew? We were young; who would have thought you could spread like that? And so fast!

So, wait a minute, I've got a question for you: how is it that when you say "we," sometimes you're one of them, and other times you're one of us? I thought sainthood set you off fairly permanently from the general run of humanity.

Well, yes and no. I guess I'm some kind of divinity now, but that doesn't mean I've forgotten where I came from. And, sure, I'm guaranteed eternal life, but isn't everyone if they follow the rules?

You're asking me? I'm a Jew, I don't know how this Christian stuff works – I'm not even all that clear on the Jewish stuff to be honest with you. I'm pretty skeptical about it all, if you want to know the truth.

I don't blame you – a lot of it seems pretty outlandish if you hold it up to the light. Plus, you've got to admit, the track record's not that good.

Let's say "spotty."

Now you're just being agreeable.

I'm not usually known for that, but maybe you're right.

38 LAST WORDS

The last words she said to me as she left for work were, "Don't go back to sleep." Naturally, I went back to sleep.

"Our task as a species," said my employer, "is nothing less than the salvation of the earth from the catastrophe of nature – how can we do that if you can't even get to work on time?" I was lost for words. "I will have to let you go," he said, "you're setting a bad example."

"You talk as if I did it deliberately," I said. "Goodbye," he said.

"This is the last straw," she said when I broke the news, though, truth to tell, this was hardly the first last straw we'd encountered in our time together. But just when you begin to count on something, it seems, that's exactly when they pull the rug right out from under you. Inspired, apparently, by my boss's example, she finally let me go, too, as did the landlord soon after that (she'd been paying the rent). Naturally, the car went with her (she'd been making the payments), as did all the furniture and fixtures she'd acquired during our tenancy. The only things she left me were a table setting for one, made of Melamine, and some expired tokens for the New York City subway. I won't say she was cruel, but she was calculating: she was well aware of my loathing for the city of New York, regardless of how far away from it we lived. Of the table setting for one I will not speak here, it was an inside joke anyway, nobody else is going to understand it. Needless to say, however, it was intended as a blow, and as a blow it succeeded.

As might have been expected, I sank into squalor and defeat (it didn't help that I could no longer afford the anti-depressants) and barely had the strength to cash the welfare checks when they reluctantly began arriving. The messages of "serves you right," and "now you know how we feel" that my parents left on my answering machine did nothing to lift my spirits either, even though I knew they were doing the best they could to be supportive of their only child in his time of need. But what else could I have expected? They always liked her more than me, and it certainly wouldn't have surprised me if I'd learned she'd moved in with them after she left me in the lurch. Although, like my parents, hers made no secret of their dislike for me, it was a source of some consolation to know they liked her even less; they had even offered to "dispatch" her if she ever returned to "darken their doorway" again (their words, not mine).

But never let it be thought that I am incapable of learning a lesson from adversity, if not several. First and foremost, of course, is the importance of *promptitude*, where all good habits of industry begin. After that there's *exactitude*, though I'll be honest and admit I'm not yet entirely clear what good habits it instills, or even what it really is; following that comes *pulchritude*, which is sometimes confused with *comeliness*, but shouldn't be; and finally, *rectitude*, which, as I understand it, has something to do with the final stage of the digestive system, which culminates in the rectum.

39 I DREAMED I WAS A RETURNING DECEASED WAR VETERAN IN MY MAIDENFORM BRA

The sign said: Hanging By A Thread. By Appointment Only. I suppose I might have thought that an interesting way to end it, had I given it any thought at all. I don't doubt they have thread – synthetic, of course – that could easily bear the weight of even the most corpulent of malefactors these days, but what would be the point? Surely it was obvious to the average stunted intellect that all that had been achieved thereby was the transformation of hanging into beheading, or at least garroting. Amazing what people will do for entertainment these days. Still, it knocks reality into a cocked hat as far as I can see. Am I saying that right, cocked hat? What does that even mean, knocking something into a cocked hat? I love the way the old and incontinent express themselves, don't you? Why can't young people today take a leaf out of their book? Because they're all too busy taking drugs, that's why, or quaffing pints down at the local with their chums while they wait for the drugs to kick in. You can't fool me – I know how you lot live nowadays, if you can call that living. Residing in a block of flats are you? Sounds like a prison sentence, if you ask me: You are hereby condemned to a block of flats – forever. And don't think you don't deserve it. Here, nip down to the pub will you, Desmond, and pick me up a clean pair of knickers for the funeral – there's a dear.

I can remember a day when mustard gas was going to be the savior of mankind – likewise Agent Orange, and anti-personnel mines, and nerve gas, even neutron bombs – *they* were going to be the savior of buildings and other important infrastructure essential to the perpetuation of the war effort. What about Zyklon B, are they still using it? And whatever happened to Zyklon A? Is there a C? How far into the alphabet do you think they've gotten by now?

40 I DREAMED I WAS A WORKING GIRL

I dreamed I was a working girl, alive as you or me. Then for a while I was the structure that sits atop the Eiffel Tower or the Chrysler Building to ward off the gods of thunder and lightning. Eventually the rain and hail drove us all inside, but not without misgivings. For all it improved our comfort, it was the move inside that undid us, for it was then we began to get too big for our britches.

It was a long time before we realized what we had done, though, and in the meantime we invented love, hate and war, and work and art and religion, slavery and penury, genocide, and good food and bad. We built great cities and sweltered in them; we put men on the moon, and many more in the earth, and still spread like a cancer over the planet. All those things we did more or less without thinking, as if it were some kind of species imperative.

It had to happen, though: one day we absent-mindedly ate the hand that fed us, and promptly the pre-packaged meals simply stopped turning up on our doorsteps. In the end I couldn't take the stress and, given the opportunity to take a decent job, I grabbed it. I can't say I'm sorry, but things are a lot duller around here now, inevitably. Still, a couple of the women and I have been talking up the idea of starting a good guys' sleeper cell or something, just to stay in shape – wish us luck! As many as there are around these days, we'll have our work cut out for us if we're serious about leaving our mark.

41 WHAT TO DO WITH THE CHICHIMECAS

Well, let's start with *angular momentum*. From there we can develop a system that builds on the mathematical insights of the Pythagoreans, the Lombards, the Delcotronics, the Adventists, the watch-fob, the diligent, the recalcitrant, the irredentists, the analects, the doppelgangers, the tremulous, the fabulists, Ma Barker, Hopalong Cassidy, pin the tail on the donkey, Lost Horizons, Lord Herringbone, duck duck goose, the wombat, the linchpin, the archfiend, poopypants, Till Eulenspiegel – stop me if I've . . .

42 NOT WITH A BANG

Step by step we have built up our resistance; the recalcitrants, undaunted, meet us by the railroad tracks. Sunrise, sunset, then sunrise and sunset again. How we tremble as the shadows lengthen – what we wouldn't give to make the days last longer, to recapture our squandered youth. Keep your teeth in a glass jar by the door, they said, in case you have to leave in a hurry. But where would we go? The expeditionary forces have already marked out all the temperate zones – beyond this you're on your own, they said, but there is no beyond any longer. Swimming in a sea of statistics, we find the establishment of the earthly empire of little use against the rain, the wind and the cold. How briefly the planet broiled after all. Now, even when we huddle together, precious heat is lost every time we think for ourselves. The stars come and go, but the sun remains elusive, forever orbiting our intractable void in search of the watchwords that might send our matchless hearts spinning off into the ether.

43 I DREAMED I WAS ALIVE

I dreamed I was alive. I was young, much younger than I am now, and I was expecting a visitor, watching apprehensively from a window, listening to a radio program and the sound of rain spattering the glass. In the past I might have been content to leave it at that, but now I felt compelled to push on. There was an enormous four-engined World War II aircraft parked at the bottom of the garden, sunlight glinting weakly off the cockpit glass, and all around it the vegetation green and lush from the rain. I passed under the starboard wing and emerged into an open field stretching to a distant hedgerow that was punctuated intermittently by magnificent oak trees.

I had written a letter to my relations explaining my sudden departure; they had burned it, along with all my books, clothes and anything else that might remind them of me. I was thankful my suffering would be short lived; theirs, I knew, would be much more enduring. But I knew that nothing of value is gained without surrendering to loss, and so I drew my raincoat tight around me and continued on. I came to a slight depression in the land, a small hollow or vale, which nonetheless seemed to expand as I descended into it, until soon I could see neither where I had come from nor where I was going.

The day wore on, the sun now traversing the sky, and the shadows lengthened as it inched slowly toward the horizon. Soon it would be night, and the only light would be the moon and stars. I watched as the sky blazed crimson, and craned my neck to follow the flight of the last birds into the sunset. Try as I may, I could not for the life of me remember what it was I had set out to do.

44 THE LAST WORD

One more word and then the show is over. No, don't ask for more, there is no more. Don't you think if I had more to say I'd say it? When have you known me to stop short?

The world's words are exhausted. I'm serious. That's not to say people won't go on talking: you know as well as I do you can't shut them up. It's just that from here on out they'll only be repeating themselves. Why? Because there aren't going to be any more new words. It had to stop somewhere, you knew infinity was just a concept; there's no evidence anywhere of anything that doesn't eventually stop or run down or run out – even infinite space is not infinite anymore. So, unless language means more to you than you're letting on, you may as well get used to the idea that we've said about all there is to say, or, at least, all there is worth saying. Of course, if you're one of those people in love with the sound of their own voice, this is not going to be an easy pill to swallow, though swallow it, inevitably, you must.

Best way to start out? Listen to yourself. Sure, your vocabulary is going to take a beating, but it's also going to be more rarified; and, yes, you'll be talking a lot less, but the chances you might actually say something meaningful will grow exponentially! Eventually, just before it all runs out, you'll be declaiming some of the last remaining jewels of the language. And when they're gone, it will all be just mystery and enigma, only without those words to name it.

45 **THE END**

I was pronounced dead. What did I know? I'd never even been sick before, let alone dead. Still, I thought I would recognize the symptoms at least. No such luck. They had to send a letter informing me, otherwise I'd never have known. The little boy down the street read it to me. There was an awkward silence, then he burst into tears. I loved you so, he blubbered, what will I do without you? I don't know, I said, I've never been dead before. Soon we were both blubbering. Can't we just go back to things as they were? I cried. Oh no, he said, my parents would never hear of it – they didn't like you all that much when you were alive. Well, at least now they needn't fear I'll molest you, I said. He was silent again for a few moments. You know, he said, I don't miss you as much as I thought I would. It's early days yet, I said, give it time. Somebody should bury you, he replied, before you start to smell. I asked him if he would do it. I'd have to do it when you weren't looking, he said. I'd probably have to hit you on the head with a shovel, to keep you from wriggling around. You don't have to worry about me wriggling, I said, I'm dead. Who's that behind you? he said. Where? I said. There, he said. I turned around to see and he hit me on the head with a shovel.

46 THE OTHER END

Let's say you're crossing a desert, a vast and ancient desert, when, to your surprise, you come across one of those lost cities people so often talk about, stark and empty, in the middle of nowhere.

You're traveling alone, of course, largely because nobody with any sense is willing to accompany you on a passage they know can result only in death or madness. Moreover, you're traveling on foot because you yourself refuse to condemn an innocent pack animal to your fate just because you are obstinate enough – or naive enough – to think you can come out on the other side alive.

In the city, the remaining buildings, where they are not eroded completely, are filled with the relentlessly drifting sand. Nobody could live here now – it's hardly possible to imagine that anyone could *ever* have lived here, as bare and ruined as the city and its surroundings are. For some inexplicable reason, though, the conviction begins to grow, slow but steady within you, that you have finally arrived at the point where it no longer makes any sense for you to travel farther; that you have, in other words, come to the end of your journey. But how is this even possible?

It's not as if you are old, or infirm, or have given up; it's not as if you have traveled to even one tenth of the places you hoped to see in your lifetime. Yet by now the conviction seems so irresistible that you're rapidly losing the capacity to even imagine resisting it; when you try to conjure any one of the numerous arguments against remaining in this spiritless spirit world, nothing comes. In fact, even as you struggle to say out loud the words your mind refuses to release to you, you feel the ability to form thoughts and ideas run through your outstretched fingers and scatter endlessly out into the ether.

All that's left now is sensation – the sunlight on your skin, the heat, the stinging sand whipped across your face, the near-silent roar of the desert's ceaseless movement. If only you could lie down, that's really all you want to do, so why not do it, why not just lie back in the sand, motionless, forever, staring up into the electric blue, until even that wordless vista has become nothing but a sea of stars against the impenetrable blackness and the sensation of sinking becomes inseparable from the giddy swirl of your ascent into the night sky as you stand calmly watching yourself disappear into the oblivion.

AC • KNOW • LEDGE • MENTS

First and foremost, my eternal gratitude and boundless appreciation go out to Ralph Franklin, Lorraine Perlman, and Peter Werbe – fondly dubbed the LOS Brain Trust – without whose unstinting support, encouragement and generosity this book would quite literally never have seen the light of day. Similarly, behind them comes a phalanx (forgive the military metaphor) of like minded individuals whose advice, close readings, publication support and wonderful, healthful meals (!) kept me going whenever my spirits began to flag. Chief among these are: Rick London, Chris and George Tysh, Kimberly Brown, Christine Monhollen, Shannon O'Brien, Al Benchich, and Rebecca Mazzei. Needless to say, the efforts of each of these folks improved the process markedly, so any remaining flaws must be, of necessity, entirely my responsibility. Finally, extra-special thank yous to my brother, Ralph, whose commitment to this project took him well above and beyond the call of mere familial duty to his occasionally feckless brother.